DELTA

ECHO

FOXTROT

INDIA

JULIET

NOVEMBER

OSCAR

PAPA

SIERRA

TANGO

X-RAY

YANKEE

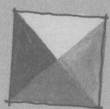

ZULU

Beatrice Zinker

UPSIDE DOWN THINKER

INCOGNITO

Beatrice Zinker

UPSIDE DOWN THINKER

INCOGNITO

by Shelley Johannes

DISNEY • HYPERION

LOS ANGELES   NEW YORK

First Edition, September 2018
10 9 8 7 6 5 4 3 2 1
FAC-020093-18215
Printed in the United States of America

This book is set in Amsterdamer Garamont Pro/Fontspring
Designed by Mary Claire Cruz and Shelley Johannes
Illustrations created with felt-tip pen, brush marker, and colored pencil on tracing paper

Library of Congress Cataloging-in-Publication Data
Names: Johannes, Shelley, author, illustrator.
Title: Incognito / by Shelley Johannes.
Description: First edition. • Los Angeles ; New York : Disney-Hyperion, 2018. •
Series: Beatrice Zinker, upside down thinker ; [2] • Summary: "Beatrice
Zinker's Operation Upside is finally in full swing, but when her
overenthusiasm puts the mission in jeopardy, she'll have to do her best to
lie low for awhile—which, for Beatrice, is not going to be easy"—
Provided by publisher.
Identifiers: LCCN 2018014930 • ISBN 9781484767399 (hardcover) •
ISBN 148476739X (hardcover)
Subjects: • CYAC: Attitude (Psychology)—Fiction. • Friendship—
Fiction. • Schools—Fiction. • Humorous stories.
Classification: LCC PZ7.1.J58 Inc 2018 • DDC [Fic]—dc23
LC record available at https://lccn.loc.gov/2018014930

ISBN 978-1-4847-6739-9 (hardcover)
ISBN 978-1-4847-6815-0 (paperback)

Reinforced binding
Visit www.DisneyBooks.com

For Nolan

Beatrice Zinker

UPSIDE DOWN THINKER

INCOGNITO

Beatrice Zinker tried to relax.

Her sister, Kate, insisted the bus ride was taking exactly as long as it always took, but today it felt like forever.

Beatrice pressed her face to the window, waiting for William Charles Elementary to come into view. As the bus bumped along, all she could think about was the secret in her backpack—and how excited she was to show Lenny.

Lenny Santos was a lot of things.

Beatrice's best friend. Her double.

And her partner in trouble.

She was also the other half of Operation Upside.

It was the second week of third grade, and—even though Operation Upside had officially begun last week—their secret plan was just getting started.

When the bus finally hissed to a stop in the parking lot, Beatrice was the first one standing. She hoisted her backpack, squeezed down the aisle, and rushed through the morning crowd.

Lenny was already waiting in their meeting spot.

"Hurry! Hurry!" said Lenny, waving frantically from the limbs of a leafy maple. "Before he sees you!"

Her hand reached out of the branches and hauled Beatrice to safety.

"Who are we spying on?" Beatrice whispered.

"Wes," Lenny mouthed. "By the door."

"Wes Carver?"

"There's only one Wes," said Lenny.

Beatrice knew just two things about Wes Carver. His pockets were always stuffed with art supplies, and he spent every recess digging for rocks at the edge of the playground.

"Look at his face," Lenny sighed. "He stands there every day, holding the door, and no one ever notices. They walk by like he's not even there."

She reached for her backpack. "I hope you don't mind, but I made him an UPSIDE."

Lenny pulled an award from her bag.

"Wow," said Beatrice. "It looks so professional."

"I used my new stencil set," Lenny replied. She adjusted her glasses, staring at the door. "I know the next award was supposed to be for Chloe, but—what if Wes needs it more?"

A giant smile lit Beatrice's face.

"Who says we have to limit ourselves? We could make a lot of people happy this week!"

Beatrice opened her bag and showed Lenny her surprise.

"Whoa," said Lenny.

"I know!" Beatrice laughed.

Eager-fingered, Lenny flipped through the stack. She shuffled through the pile once, then—eyebrows crinkled—she shuffled again.

"Wait," she said. "They're all blank?"

Excitement buzzed through Beatrice.

There were ten of them, and they were all the same. Crisp, white, and waiting for a name.

"They won't be blank for long," she said.

Below them, an endless trail of students moved down the sunny sidewalk. Friends and strangers. Kindergartners, classmates—even fifth-graders.

Lenny passed the pile back to Beatrice. "Do you have any ideas?"

Beatrice grinned, her smile full of ideas. "I have one or two. . . ."

Lenny smiled back. "I bet you do." Her finger traced Wes's award, while Beatrice packed the others away. "At least we know exactly who's getting mine today."

Just then, the morning bell rang.

On the count of three, they zipped their bags, zipped their lips, and dropped from the tree. Together they marched across the lawn and ducked inside, with a friendly nod to Wes Carver as they passed by.

Beatrice's feet skipped in anticipation.

The second week of Operation Upside was going to be even better than the first.

2

Beatrice headed toward Classroom 3B with a pep in her step. She had a backpack full of possibilities and Lenny by her side. This week, nothing could stop Operation Upside.

"STOP!" a booming voice bellowed down the hall. The blast of a whistle shrilled like an alarm. "No running! Absolutely not."

Only one person had a voice like that.

And a whistle permanently snaked around her neck.

HER ⟶

Mrs. Tamarack, Beatrice's third-grade teacher, stood guard outside their classroom with her arms folded across her chest and her eyes locked on Lenny and Beatrice. Every head in the hall turned and looked at them too.

Beatrice glanced at her feet, then at Lenny's.

Technically, they were skipping.

"Rules are rules for a reason, girls," said Mrs. Tamarack when they got close. Her whistle glinted in her fist. "No shenanigans. No upside down antics. Do you need a reminder that you get three warnings before I take recess away?"

Beatrice shook her head. She didn't need a reminder.

If there were an award for the strictest person in the world, Evelyn Tamarack would definitely win it—and she'd probably keep the trophy on the corner of her desk, and polish it every minute.

MOST STRICT
EVELYN TAMARACK

Beatrice's fingers wriggled around the straps of her backpack. A smile tugged at her lips.

Mrs. Tamarack's eyebrows crinkled in irritation. "Did I say something funny, Beatrice?"

"No!" said Beatrice, covering her mouth. "Sometimes I smile when I'm nervous. . . ."

Or when a really good idea pops into my head, she thought.

Lenny grabbed her arm and hauled her through the door before Beatrice could say anything more. With her back to her teacher, Beatrice shifted into secret-mission mode. She could already imagine Mrs. Tamarack's name spelled out in bold, glittering gold.

Chloe Llewelyn leapt from her seat, squealing, as they entered the room. "Lenny!" she said, waving a fuzzy headband in the air. "Look what Parvati brought!"

Chloe and Lenny were next-door neighbors. The Llewelyns had moved into the neighborhood over the summer, just before school started. Chloe had only been at William Charles Elementary for a week—but like today's bus ride, it felt like forever.

From across the room, Parvati waved hi.

Grace and Eva meowed hello.

An assortment of pointy ears poked out of their hair.

"I raided my sister's dress-up box," Parvati explained. "Aren't they *purr*-fect?"

"And," said Chloe, "my mom gave us her old stethoscopes." She curled a spare one around Lenny's neck, and smiled at the effect.

"This is so cool," said Lenny. She stuck the earbuds in place and tested them out. "It's like we're real veterinarians now."

When Chloe started her veterinary clinic at recess last week, Beatrice assumed everyone would get bored in a day or two.

Instead, every recess, more people showed up at the back of the playground, crawling on all fours, woofing and whimpering for medical assistance.

Now they had fuzzy headbands.

And working stethoscopes.

Chloe nudged Beatrice's shoulder. "Want some cat ears, Beatrice?"

CAT EARS, NOT BAT EARS!

"Maybe later," said Beatrice. She couldn't think about the vet clinic right now.

She was a spy on a mission.

She needed to focus.

Classroom 3B was buzzing with distractions. Mrs. Tamarack ran a tight ship, but the first few minutes of every day were complete chaos. The room was a whirlwind of binders and backpacks, lunches and last-minute questions, homework and stories from the weekend.

Conditions couldn't be more perfect.

Non-spies don't realize it, but most secret missions are not accomplished in secret at all. Most operations happen out in the open, with real life swirling all around them.

Chaos is a spy's best friend.

As Beatrice's other best friend checked the heartbeats of several eager cats, Beatrice seized the moment. She skirted around Lenny and her new stethoscope, and rushed to her desk.

Time was limited, so Beatrice worked fast.

She pulled an award from her backpack, fished a marker from her pencil pouch— then, left-handed, she disguised her writing and filled in the blanks with quick, sparkling strokes.

In the middle of real life, while everyone was doing their thing, Beatrice calmly blew the ink dry, coolly walked across the room, and casually slipped Mrs. Tamarack's award into the homework bin with everyone's math.

Mission accomplished—just like that.

Mrs. Tamarack clapped her hands and blinked the lights. "One, two, three—eyes on me," she called out. "Contrary to popular belief, this classroom is not a zoo." She pointed at Lenny, Chloe, and the fuzzy headband crew. "Veterinary clinic—this means you."

Beatrice sidestepped back to her seat, feeling triumphant. Class hadn't started yet, and the first UPSIDE of the week was already in motion.

3

Beatrice's moment of triumph did not last long. It ended the moment Mrs. Tamarack frowned and looked her way.

THAT'S ONE

I'M FIXING MY BUN!

She seemed determined to take recess away.

Mrs. Tamarack's second warning came during morning announcements.

It surprised Beatrice as much as her sneeze.

Thirty minutes later, Mrs. Tamarack shouted warning three.

The room emptied for morning recess right before lunch.

Sunlight poured through the open door as fifty feet raced outside, and the playground filled with happy screams. Mrs. Tamarack cleared her throat and squinted at Beatrice—a wordless reminder to stay in her seat.

Behind Beatrice, another throat cleared, and someone shyly tapped her sleeve.

A pair of cat ears dropped onto her desk.

"We brought you these," said Chloe.

"So you can *pretend* you're outside, at least," said Lenny.

Mrs. Tamarack raised an eyebrow in their direction. "Recess is now or never, girls."

The girls quickly chose now.

Beatrice slumped in her seat as she watched them leave.

"Don't mope," said Mrs. Tamarack. "I'm certain there's homework you can do."

At the mention of homework, Beatrice's eyes flew across the room and landed on the wire basket. The crisp edge of Mrs. Tamarack's award winked at her from its hiding spot, where it waited patiently to be found.

Beatrice sat up straight and beamed.

Her first recess was gone, but the day was going better than it seemed.

Except, after lunch, Mrs. Tamarack's mood was even worse.

Beatrice lost second recess even faster than she'd lost the first.

Beatrice's face remained calm as she returned to her seat, but inside . . .

OUTSIDE

INSIDE!

. . . she was cartwheeling.

If anyone needed an UPSIDE today, it was Mrs. Tamarack. Her teacher was in the worst mood ever, and just a few feet away, buried in a pile of math facts, was a piece of paper with her name on it.

It was only a matter of time before Operation Upside made Mrs. Tamarack's day.

GUARANTEED SMILE

THINK! TWICE.

If your name's not on it, I don't want it!

HOMEWORK

Beatrice sucked in her cheeks to keep the smile off her face.

She was the cofounder of a secret operation. Being a spy required endurance, even when endurance was hard.

All afternoon, Mrs. Tamarack
click-clacked and clip-clopped
this way and that, completely
ignoring the homework stack.
Once, she paused.
Twice, she even glanced.
But each time was only
happenstance.

The wait dragged on through Science, stretched
into Social Studies, and ran all the way into second
recess with the rest of the class.

Beatrice waited, stuck in her chair, until the
very last minute of the day, when Mrs. Tamarack
finally made her move.

While everyone was crowding the door, with
backpacked shoulders and restless feet, Mrs.
Tamarack strode across the room and stacked
their homework, nice and neat.

Victory!

"Last call," she announced, waving the papers over her head. When no one responded, she tucked the pile—award and all—into the tote bag under her seat.

The final bell rang just as the bag hit the floor.

Beatrice threw her own bag over her shoulder and flounced toward the door.

Her backpack felt a touch lighter than when she'd walked in, and she floated into the corridor like she was walking on air.

She was guaranteed to see Mrs. Tamarack's smile tomorrow. And if she hurried—she'd get to see Lenny's smile even sooner.

4

The other half of Operation Upside was already halfway down the hall when Beatrice caught her sleeve. Lenny told Chloe she'd meet her on the bus, then hung back and slowed her pace.

"Mrs. Tamarack was in a mood today, huh?" said Lenny.

"You're telling me," Beatrice replied.

Lenny shivered. "I was afraid to move. I can only imagine how it was for you."

"Actually," said Beatrice, "it was a pretty good day." She looked around, then lowered her voice. In a confidential tone, she gave Lenny the victorious, top-secret play-by-play.

Lenny didn't smile, or clap, or jump around, like Beatrice imagined she would.

Instead her shoes squeaked to a stop.

In the middle of the crowded corridor, Lenny gaped at her, wide-eyed and pale. *"MOST STRICT?!"* she repeated in a heated whisper. "That's really what you wrote?"

It's hard to be an upside down thinker if you second-guess yourself all the time, but the horror on Lenny's face was impossible to ignore.

As the stream of traffic diverged around them, Beatrice felt her first prickle of doubt.

"What?" she asked, trying to shrug it off. "She's really good at being strict."

Lenny groaned. "You're going to be in so much trouble, Beatrice." Chewing her lip, she snuck a glance at Classroom 3B. It was just a dot at the end of the hallway now. "Can we get it back?"

"It's in Mrs. Tamarack's tote bag," Beatrice told her. "Mixed in with the math."

Lenny's shoulders slumped.

A teacher's tote bag was forbidden territory—even for Operation Upside.

They traveled the rest of the corridor in silence, Beatrice thinking, Lenny slinking.

When they reached the end, the door swung wide. Wes Carver's friendly face peeked around from the other side.

"Yikes," he said, when they stepped into the light. "You look like you need some cheering up."

He reached into his sweatshirt pocket and dug around. His search continued from pocket to pocket to pocket as an impressive variety of markers spilled to the ground.

For a moment, Beatrice stopped thinking.

Lenny stopped slinking.

Their heads tilted in curiosity as they watched Wes hunt for cheer.

"Here!" he finally announced, fists raised above his head and art supplies scattered at his feet.

With the flair of a new magician, he dropped something into each of their outstretched hands.

Rocks.
With a message
on them.

"Thanks!" Beatrice
grinned.
"Yes, thank you, Wes,"
said Lenny, not looking cheered up at all.

As they joined the jam-packed pathway, Lenny
lifted her rock to her nose. "I think he used scented
markers. Mine smells just like licorice."
Lenny passed her rock to Beatrice.

Lenny was right.

It smelled exactly like licorice.

Beatrice smelled her own and smiled—it was pineapple. Like upside down cake.

Lenny sighed. "I *really* wanted Wes to get an UPSIDE. . . ." Opening her bag, she flashed Wes's perfectly stenciled certificate at Beatrice. "I can't even carry this around," she said. "It's too risky now. Once Mrs. Tamarack sees her award, Operation Upside is doomed."

Beatrice tucked Wes's award into her backpack. "Operation Upside is not doomed." Certainty swelled up as Beatrice said the words. "It was a top-secret mission. Even if Mrs. Tamarack hates her award, we'll be fine. She'll never know it was me."

The schoolyard was thinning out as the buses filled up.

Lenny pinned Beatrice in a sideways stare. "No offense—but look at you."

Lenny had a point.

And Mrs. Tamarack looked at her constantly.

"Get a good look now," said Beatrice, suddenly knowing exactly what to do. To be safe, she would lie low for a day or two. "Tomorrow I'm going incognito."

Lenny wrinkled her nose.

"What's incognito?"

"You'll see," said Beatrice. "Just wear one of your sparkly sweaters, and keep an eye out for me."

Operation Upside wasn't over yet.

Beatrice was more certain than ever.

Instead of upside down, she just needed to go deeper undercover.

5

The next morning, Beatrice's sister marched out of their bedroom closet with a hanger on each hand. "What do you think?" Kate asked. "Should I wear this or this?"

this?

this?

The choice was obvious, but before Beatrice could open her mouth, Kate was opening hers again.

"Whoa," she said, pointing at Beatrice's outfit, "are you wearing all that pink on purpose?"

Isn't it PERFECT?

"Wait a minute." Kate stepped closer. "Are you wearing ninja pants under that dress?" Beatrice ignored her sister and marched to the window, binoculars in hand. The less Kate knew about her plans, the better.

LYING LOW UNIFORM

THINKING CAP 2.0

BINOCULARS

NINJA PANTS?

"Please don't do anything crazy," Kate begged. "Foreign Language Club starts today, remember?"

It was impossible to forget.

Kate was president of the Foreign Language Club at William Charles Elementary. She'd practiced her welcome speech late into the night, and had been pacing their bedroom floor, whispering in French, since the sun came up.

Beatrice positioned her binoculars against the window. "Just a sec," she told Kate. She squinted her eyes and twisted the dials, frowning.

Everything was blurry.

Dropping the binoculars, Beatrice wiped the window with her arm. Her nose pressed against the glass. "Wow," she breathed.

"Wow, what?" Kate wanted to know.

There was nothing but fog in every direction. Clouds hovered over the street like cotton candy. It looked like the sky was upside down.

Beatrice fitted the binoculars back to her face, squinting at the view. Scrappy, her neighbor's cat, strolled out of the nothingness, right on cue. Scrappy's red leash materialized out of the fog right behind her.

Beatrice smiled, waiting to see her neighbor, Mrs. Jenkins, appear on the other end. Beatrice always had a good day when she saw Mrs. Jenkins walking Scrappy.

But Mrs. Jenkins didn't step out of the fog.

Instead—the fog produced a girl.

Long dark hair and tendrils of fog blocked the girl's face, but Beatrice still recognized her.

It was Sam Darzi, the third-grader who lived in the house across the street.

Her walk was unmistakable.

She shuffled down the sidewalk with her head down, her shoulders slumped, and her too-big black boots scuffing against the pavement.

They disappeared into the mist in the same order they appeared.

First Scrappy.

Then the leash.

Then Sam Darzi.

Beatrice squinched her face and turned the binocular dials, trying to make sense of what she'd seen. Where was Mrs. Jenkins? And why was Sam Darzi walking her cat?

"It's not raining, is it?" Kate edged closer, peeking over Beatrice's shoulder.

Beatrice dropped the blinds.

"No," she said, "but it's very mysterious." She pointed to the hanger on the right. "I'd go with the cape."

"Huh?" said Kate, confused. She looked at her hangers and heaved a sigh. "It's not a cape, Beatrice—it's a *poncho.*"

Beatrice looped her binoculars over the bedpost. "Is *poncho* the French word for cape?"

Kate huffed back to the closet, mumbling something Beatrice couldn't hear.

When her sister reappeared, the cape was missing. She was wearing a red blazer with a flowered scarf instead.

Kate gestured toward the stairs. "Ready?"

Though the day had started strangely—with Sam, and the fog, and missing Mrs. Jenkins—none of that changed Beatrice's plan. She knew exactly what she needed to do.

She hiked up her ninja pants, smoothed the hem of her skirt, and flashed a smile at her sister.

"Ready," she said.

She was as ready as she'd ever be to wear a pink dress on purpose.

6

"Oh, Beatrice!" her mother, Nancy Zinker, cried from the kitchen doorway.

Her hand flew to her heart.

"You look adorable."

She elbowed her husband. "Doesn't she look adorable, Pete?"

Pete Zinker assessed his pink-clad daughter.

"She looks like a girl with a plan," he decided.

He tossed Beatrice a granola bar, which she caught in the air.

"I'm just lying low today," Beatrice said, trying to play it cool.

A swirl of red twirled in from the stair.

"What about me?" said Kate. "How do I look?"

"Spot-on," her dad declared, doling out another granola bar. "Perfectly presidential."

"No big breakfast this morning, girls," said Nancy Zinker, fussing over Kate. "We don't want to risk ruining your outfit." She rearranged Kate's scarf until it was fluffed and knotted just like hers.

"I couldn't eat anyway," said Kate. "I'm *très nerveuse.*"

"There's no need to be nervous," said her mother. "You'll be great!"

Pete Zinker pulled out a chair at the table. "One more practice round?"

Kate's eyes lit up. *"Oui!"* she said, pulling out her flash cards. *"Merci!"*

Beatrice scanned the room for an exit. "Has anyone seen Henry?"

"He's watching one of his shows," said her dad. "Want to keep him company?"

"Es-yay!" said Beatrice, as she made her escape.

KINKAJOU

KING | KAH | JOO

Beatrice found her baby brother on the living room rug, smiling at the television. On-screen, a furry creature was swinging upside down by its tail.

Some babies love cartoons.

Henry Zinker adored documentaries.

Today's starred the kinkajous of South America.

"Oh!" said Beatrice, plopping next to him. "I love these guys!"

She bit into her breakfast.

"I wish I was a kinkajou," she sighed.

While Kate hung out in the kitchen, rehearsing with an audience of two, Beatrice and Henry flipped upside down and pretended to be kinkajous.

Pete Zinker peeked into the living room as the rain forest faded and the credits started scrolling.

A huge smile brightened his face.

"There's the Beatrice I know!" He laughed and then held up her backpack. "Time to go, Miss Lying Low."

Beatrice jumped to her feet and straightened her skirt.

Her dad squashed her in a hug. "Keep that chin up, buttercup," he said. "Whatever you've got planned."

"I will," said Beatrice.

Slinging her backpack over her shoulder, she stepped into the morning fog. Incognito, in her pink dress, Beatrice felt more unstoppable than ever.

Beatrice kept her chin up the whole bus ride.

Instead of hopping off, like she usually did, she matched Kate's careful steps into the slow-moving crowd.

A sparkly sweater emerged from the haze. "Beatrice?"

Lenny blinked at Beatrice through the fog.

"Well," said Beatrice, "what do you think?"

"Wow," Lenny replied.

"That's a lot of pink."

A LOT!

"My closet's full of this stuff," said Beatrice. "I could go incognito for weeks, maybe months, and my mom wouldn't even have to do laundry!"

Curious heads turned in their direction.

Lenny's eyes darted around. "This way," she said, angling off the path. "It's dangerous out here."

"The bushes!" said Beatrice, diving for cover behind a row of hedges.

Lenny crouched next to her and frowned at Beatrice's pink ensemble. "This is your plan?"

"This the backup plan," Beatrice clarified. "It's still possible Mrs. Tamarack is going to like her award. Once we see her happy smile, we can sneak Wes his award by the end of the day."

Beatrice paused for effect.

"That's the real plan."

Beatrice wasn't sure she believed it herself anymore, but she had to hope.

Lenny pulled a branch aside and they both peeked through the leaves. Wes Carver was standing at the door, just like yesterday, holding it politely as everyone walked inside.

Lenny chewed her thumbnail.

Doubt filled her eyes.

"Don't worry, though," Beatrice assured her. "No matter what, I'll be the picture of lying low."

"I don't think that's possible for you," said Lenny, laughing. "Without a major miracle or something!"

Beatrice hopped to her feet and dusted herself off. "Anything's possible with the right costume."

She looped her sleeve through Lenny's and popped out of the bushes to prove her point. "Pink is the perfect camouflage."

Arm in arm, they bounded down the busy sidewalk. "See?" said Beatrice. "I'm practically invisible."

"Beatrice!" a voice shouted across the plaza. "Lenny!" it yelled. "Wait up!"

Chloe Llewelyn strolled out of the fog, flagging them down. Her smile beamed through the haze as she skipped to their side. "Are you guys excited for lunch?"

Lenny's hand flew to her mouth. "I almost forgot!"

"You never forget stuffed-crust pizza day," said Beatrice.

Stuffed-crust pizza day was their favorite.

"I wasn't talking about pizza," said Chloe. She lifted her monogrammed lunch bag. "I meant Foreign Language Club—it starts at lunch today!"

Beatrice peeked into her backpack. Her own lunch bag was tucked up front, where her mother always put it. No one had told her Kate's club meant missing her favorite lunch.

"Je suis impatiente!" Chloe exclaimed, clapping with excitement. A ring of flash cards dangled from her finger. "That means *I can't wait* in French. I've been practicing."

It was eerie.

Kate and Chloe were practically twins.

Chloe pointed at Beatrice. "I see you dressed up for it. Like *moi.*"

Beatrice stared at her own dress, then stared back at Chloe's.

Lenny laughed, way too delighted.
"You're twins!"

"*Jumelles!*" Chloe said, crushing
Beatrice in a hug.

THAT MEANS
TWINS IN
FRENCH!

This was not part of the plan.
It was not part of the backup plan either.

Maybe Lenny was right, and she *did* need a miracle today.

Beatrice crossed her fingers for luck as they ducked past Wes and went inside. Hopefully yesterday's UPSIDE had already worked its magic, and the miracle of Mrs. Tamarack's happy smile would greet them at the door.

8

Just before the bell, the pink-dress parade entered Classroom 3B, with Chloe leading the way. Sam Darzi slipped through the door right behind them.

Mrs. Tamarack and her miraculous smile were nowhere in sight.

"Guys!" Parvati shouted across the room. "Look what we have today!"

Beatrice didn't have time to see the veterinary prop-of-the-day.

Her mysterious cat-walking neighbor required her full attention.

Sam Darzi was heading for the coat closet. A worn yellow backpack slouched down her shoulder as her boots scuffed across the carpet. Long black laces dragged behind her.

Beatrice hadn't given Sam much thought before today. But after spying her in the fog with Mrs. Jenkins's cat, she had so many questions.

The Darzi family moved in almost a year ago. Sam enrolled at William Charles Elementary a few weeks into second grade, but even now, no one knew much about her.

Not even Lenny.

And Lenny knew everyone.

Without warning, the classroom door slammed. Mrs. Tamarack stood in the doorway, tote bag in hand. "Seats, everyone! Seats!"

Lenny rushed past and plopped into her desk by the door. Beatrice hurried to her front-row seat and dropped her bag on the floor.

Evelyn Tamarack was not smiling.

"One, two, three—eyes on me!"

Everyone faced forward as Mrs. Tamarack planted herself at the center of the room and snapped her fingers at the boys in the back. Then she raised her voice and addressed the class.

"Apparently, someone thought they were being funny yesterday."

Her palm slapped a piece of paper onto Beatrice's desk. Just inches away, trapped under Mrs. Tamarack's hand, was her UPSIDE award. The words MOST STRICT peeked between her fingers.

"Needless to say—I was not amused." Mrs. Tamarack suspended the award in her fingertips, like a piece of litter she didn't want to touch. "Not amused at all."

Beatrice wasn't trying to be funny.

She was trying to be a force for good.

Her teacher marched across the room and taped the award above the pencil sharpener. "If anyone has any information, I trust you'll follow the instructions and do the right thing."

Beatrice snuck a glance at Lenny, whose eyes narrowed accusingly.

Her face was bright pink.

During the long morning that followed, Lenny spent her spare time staring at the ominous poster above the pencil sharpener.

Beatrice spent her morning trying to look on the upside instead.

Mrs. Tamarack's reaction wasn't the best-case scenario.

But it also wasn't the worst.

Despite the WANTED sign, the identity of Operation Upside was still a secret. Mrs. Tamarack had no idea who was responsible for her award. And Beatrice would make sure she never would. She was going to be on her best, pink-dressed behavior.

Being a wanted criminal was very motivating.

It might even be the miracle she needed.

9

Beatrice stayed under Mrs. Tamarack's radar all morning.

When her knee itched, she didn't scratch.

When she had a question, she didn't ask.

When she knew an answer, she didn't interrupt. When she dropped her pencil, she let it roll all the way down the aisle, where Wes Carver kindly picked it up.

No matter how many good ideas popped into her head, Beatrice didn't share them.

She didn't cough.

She didn't sneeze.

She didn't do a thing when her legs fell asleep.

By the time the door swung open for recess, she felt like a prisoner set free. Beatrice hurried to the back of the playground, into the branches of her favorite tree. Hanging from its familiar limbs, she could finally breathe.

It was perfect recess weather.

Fog hovered over the playground like a ghost.

There were endless games to play in the morning mist. Beatrice had so many ideas, she made a list.

"Should I sign you up, Beatrice?" Chloe came out of the haze with Parvati at her side. A clipboard was balanced in the crook of her arm. "Are you playing today?"

GHOST TAG
CAPTURE THE FLAG
TROPICAL SAFARI
Mist
ARCTIC EXPLORERS
ZOMBIE APOCALYPSE!!

While Chloe flipped open her patient list, Beatrice looked over her own. "Want to play Zombie Apocalypse?" Beatrice asked.

Chloe cringed. "Zombies eat brains."

Parvati held up a fuzzy gray headband. "We could use another cat."

Beatrice wrinkled her nose.

"I was a cat on Friday," she said. "I could be a kinkajou. . . ."

KEEEK!

"I've never even heard of that," said Chloe. Her pen tapped the clipboard. "It's not another bat, is it?"

Last time Beatrice was a bat, recess ended with a bloody nose—and Chloe almost passed out. For a veterinarian, Chloe was surprisingly squeamish.

"It's not a bat," Beatrice told her. "It's related to the raccoon, but I think it looks more like a mongoose."

Chloe grimaced. "Raccoons eat garbage."

"Kinkajous just eat fruit," Beatrice informed her. "Sometimes birds and bugs—but *mostly* fruit."

Chloe paled and pointed at the posters behind her.

"Sorry, Beatrice . . ."

Beatrice shrugged.

"That's okay—I won't need a vet anyway. Kinkajous are very hardy animals. Did you know they can turn their feet backward to escape danger?"

A hint of green splotched Chloe's cheeks.

"I'd better go," she said, already turning around. She rushed into the clinic, walking forward as fast as her feet would take her. Parvati hurried after her, waving good-bye.

Lenny came out of the clinic as Chloe and Parvati went in. She was just who Beatrice was hoping to see.

"Lenny!" she exclaimed. Beatrice extended her arms and groaned convincingly. "Want to play Zombie Apocalypse with me?"

When Lenny didn't respond, Beatrice tried again. "Capture the flag?"

"There's a 'Wanted' poster, Beatrice! You're supposed to be lying low."

"I am," said Beatrice.

"This is how kinkajous lie low."

"Come play vet with me," Lenny begged.
"Please? There's safety in numbers,
and blending in with Chloe is
the perfect cover. You could
be our new assistant!"

"Don't worry," Beatrice
told her. "I'll be as boring
as possible out here on
this branch. I'll blend in
with the trees."

And Beatrice meant it.
She planned to be the
most boring kinkajou William
Charles Elementary had ever seen.

But seconds after Lenny walked
away, Wes Carver appeared out of the mist and
knocked every boring thought from her mind.

His arms were filled
with water bottles. His
pockets overflowed with
art supplies. With every
step of his bouncy stride,
a spare marker fell out of his
pocket, leaving a colorful trail behind him.

"Hey, Beatrice." Wes nodded hello. "I heard
Chloe needs an assistant."

"Lenny just stuck an ad by the door," said
Beatrice.

Chloe appeared in the doorway of the clinic. "Did I hear my name?"

Wes bounded over. Water sloshed in his arms as he trotted away. With his back to Beatrice, he greeted Chloe and offered her a bottle.

Only mumbles of their exchange floated back to Beatrice.

As Chloe tipped her head for a sip of water, Wes pointed to the poster by the door. Chloe frowned, then flipped a paper on her clipboard and began to draw.

Beatrice squinted her eyes, but she couldn't see what Chloe was doing.

A moment later, Chloe stomped her foot and glared at her pen. From her jiggle of frustration, Beatrice guessed it was out of ink.

Wes quickly offered her a handful of options.

Chloe uncapped a bright pink marker and breathed in its scent.

Beatrice wondered if it smelled like cherry. Or watermelon? Maybe bubble gum.

With fresh ink, Chloe finished easily, then stole a strip of tape from the VET sign overhead and tacked her new poster above the door. While she was still on tiptoe, a sudden wind whipped through the trees and ripped the papers free.

Chloe tried to catch them, but the signs billowed up and slipped through her fingers, twisting and dancing above the grass, just out of reach.

Chloe moaned in frustration.

Arms outstretched, spinning in circles, she chased them down.

Beatrice smiled.

It looked like Chloe was playing Zombie Apocalypse after all.

After a lot of stumbling and groaning, she finally caught the VET sign. Wes snatched the other in midair. Then, with a smile, he produced a roll of duct tape from his sleeve.

Wes Carver was the wizard of art supplies.

Unfortunately, Chloe didn't want a magician.

She anchored both papers in place with shiny strips of his silver tape and stood back for a better view.

Looking at Chloe's newest addition,
Wes gulped, Beatrice gasped, and
Chloe lifted her hands in apology.

"Rules are rules," Beatrice saw her say. Then she handed Wes his marker and tape.

His head shook, refusing to take them.

His supplies stayed like that, suspended uncertainly between them, until Chloe's lips finally moved.

"Okay," she said. "Thank you."

With fumbling fingers, she pocketed the pink marker and slipped the tape around her wrist, as Wes buried his hands in his sweatshirt and walked away.

"Bye, Beatrice," he said as he lumbered past.

"She said no?"

Wes lifted his shoulders.

He trudged through the trees with his head down and his shoulders slouched.

Beatrice forgot she was a boring kinkajou.

She forgot about her pink dress and her intentions to lie low. All she could think about was the certificate sitting at the bottom of her backpack.

The one that said WES CARVER in impressively stenciled letters.

While Wes wandered across the playground alone, plucking rocks from the grass, Beatrice crept from treetop to treetop, sneaking all the way back to class.

KINKAJOU
ON A MISSION

10

It should have been easy.

Classroom 3B was a ghost town. The entire upper elementary was outside at recess.

Beatrice didn't need to sneak.

She didn't need to tiptoe.

She didn't need any of the spy moves she'd been practicing all summer.

All she had to do was stroll over to the coat closet and slide the award into Wes Carver's mail slot.

Right side up.

In plain sight.

Like no big deal.

She'd been lying low all morning, though. The deserted classroom was the perfect opportunity to practice her moves.

THE FLAT AS A PANCAKE

HOT-LAVA LEGS

THE DON'T LOOK DOWN

THE STOP, DROP, AND ROLL

Which is how Beatrice found herself wedged in the coat closet, upside down, searching for Wes's mailbox with his award clamped between her teeth.

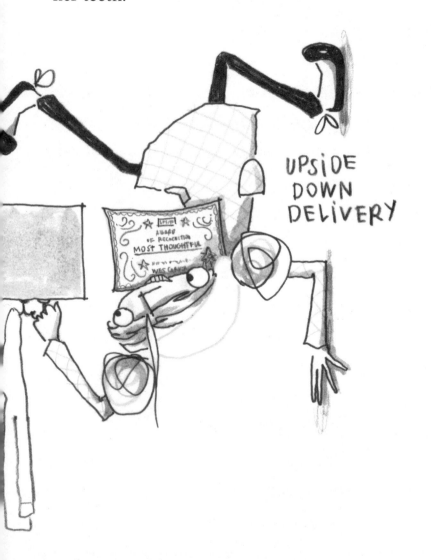

UPSIDE
DOWN
DELIVERY

Lenny's name jumped out at her first.

Chloe's was right beside it.

Two slots down from Chloe's name, Beatrice spotted Wes's.

Wes's certificate slid smoothly into the empty slot. Beatrice pictured the surprise on Wes's face when he discovered it. She imagined him reading the words Lenny had lettered in gold.

Out in the hallway, footsteps interrupted the magic of the moment.

Beatrice sucked in her breath and froze.

Listening.

It wasn't the quick, clicking walk of a teacher, or the confident steps of the custodian.

It was a slow shuffle and scuff.

As the footsteps neared the classroom, Beatrice heard humming. Still holding her breath, she waited for the sound to pass by.

But the footsteps didn't fade away.

Instead they got louder.

And the humming grew closer.

The volume continued to increase, louder and closer, until the person entered Classroom 3B, and clomped straight for the coat closet.

Beatrice inched up and out of sight just as a pair of clunky black boots came around the corner. When Beatrice recognized the dark curtain of hair, she almost fell to the floor.

For the second time that day, Beatrice found herself spying on Sam Darzi.

||

Beatrice carefully released her breath and molded herself to the surface of the ceiling.

The pounding of her heartbeat pulsed in her ears as her sweaty palms struggled to maintain their grip.

Sam strolled to the coat hooks, seeming unaware of her classmate hovering above her head.

Her boots stopped directly below Beatrice, right in front of the spot with Wes's name on it. Still humming, Sam lifted her arm and reached into Wes's mailbox.

Beatrice's mouth opened in surprise.

Sam was mysterious,
but Beatrice never
imagined she was
a thief.

Sam pulled Wes's shimmery certificate out
of the slot and turned it over in her hands. Her
forehead wrinkled in confusion.

The humming stopped.

Hooking her hair behind her ear, she scanned
the page. Beatrice had never seen Sam's whole face
before.

It was like meeting someone new.

Sam's shadowy half-moon face was replaced with a sunny full one.

Her mouth moved over the words, lingering over the biggest letters on the page—the ones that spelled out MOST THOUGHTFUL.

Then her lips did something Beatrice had never seen them do. They turned up—just a little bit—on both ends.

Beatrice couldn't believe it.

Sam Darzi was smiling.

In that moment of wonder, a bright yellow detail caught Beatrice's eye. Sam's backpack—her one-of-a-kind yellow backpack—was hanging under Wes's mailbox. The truth almost knocked Beatrice off the ceiling.

Sam wasn't standing in front of Wes's mailbox. She was standing in front of her own.

Beatrice's face felt hot.

While she was supposed to be lying low, she'd snuck into Classroom 3B and put Wes's special award in Sam Darzi's mailbox by mistake.

Beatrice knew the precise moment Sam's eyes reached the print at the bottom of the certificate. The part of the award that said: THIS UPSIDE AWARD IS PRESENTED TO WES CARVER.

The smile-stealing part.

The part that did not say SAM DARZI.

Sam blinked and shook her head. A shadow of hair swooshed back over her face and covered up the sun.

Beatrice could only see half of Sam's mouth, but it was enough to tell that her whole mouth wasn't smiling anymore.

Sam no longer looked like someone new. She looked exactly like Sam again.

Shuffling three steps to the right, her boots paused in front of Wes's real mailbox. Sam stood there, biting her lip, rolling and unrolling the certificate in her palms. Reading and rereading the words.

Beatrice barely dared to hope—maybe Sam was giving it back? Maybe she was fixing the mistake. Maybe Wes would get his award after all.

A bit of Beatrice's breath hissed out. It wasn't loud, but Sam's head snapped up. Her eyes fixed on Beatrice.

There were no words in Beatrice's brain. Even upside down, she couldn't think of the right thing to say.

Sam snatched her yellow bag and stepped backward, clutching the award to her chest.

"I just needed my backpack . . ." Sam mumbled. She took one step, then two, then four—until she had retreated completely, all the way out the door.

Sam's footsteps faded behind her.

First out of the room, then down the hall.

Until they were only a memory.

Classroom 3B was empty again, but Beatrice's mind filled with questions. What was Sam going to do with Wes's award? Did she plan to keep Beatrice's identity a secret, or turn her in to Mrs. Tamarack?

Most of all, Beatrice wondered how quickly she could get to Lenny—and how upset Lenny was going to be when she found out what Beatrice had done.

12

Chloe Llewelyn stood in the middle of the veterinary waiting room looking more like a guard dog than a doctor.

Beatrice needed to get past her fast.

Recess was almost over. Mrs. Tamarack's whistle was probably already in her lips, waiting to sound.

First—Beatrice tried casual.

"Is Lenny in back?" she asked.

Chloe checked her clipboard. "I'm sorry, but Dr. Santos is with another patient right now."

Beatrice tried not-casual.

Chloe gestured at the animals lounging around the waiting room. "Everyone's got an emergency. We're doing the best we can."

When Chloe played veterinarian, she was all in.

Beatrice collapsed on the ground and tried being all in too.

"I have Kinkajou Fever," she croaked, her arm tossed over her face. "Only Lenny can save me."

"Sorry, Beatrice—rules are rules."

"I don't think the mongoose rule applies to her," said a voice behind them.

Peeking through the waiting room window was the earnest face of Wes Carver.

Beatrice was too shocked to speak.

"Kinkajous and mongooses look a lot alike," Wes continued, "but they aren't even remotely related. Kinkajous are cousins of the raccoon."

"How do you people know this stuff?" Chloe demanded.

"I read a lot of books," said Wes. "And watch a lot of PBS."

Chloe put her hands on her hips. "My other rule still stands."

Thanks to Wes's heavy-duty duct tape, the GIRLS ONLY sign held fast above the doorway. The mongoose ban might not have excluded Beatrice, but the No Boys Allowed rule still applied to Wes.

"I know," Wes said with a shrug. "Mrs. Tamarack sent me back here to make sure you heard the five-minute whistle."

"Oh," said Chloe. She frowned at the crowded waiting room. Five minutes wasn't much time. Everyone, including Beatrice, looked up at her with hopeful eyes.

"Sure you don't need any help?" Wes offered. "I know a lot about animals."

Chloe tucked her clipboard under her arm. "We've got this under control." She curled her fist into an imaginary microphone and raised her voice. "Paging Dr. Santos! Dr. Santos to the waiting room!" Her call rang out with surprising volume. "There's a wild animal that needs to see you. She claims it's an emergency."

Beatrice jumped up and crushed Chloe in a hug. "Thank you, thank you!" she exclaimed.

Over Chloe's shoulder, Beatrice said the words one more time. "Thank you," she mouthed toward the window.

Wes gave a small smile and loped away.

"What's going on out here?" Lenny rushed into the waiting room, looking around.

Chloe rubbed her temples. "Beatrice has Kinkajou Fever."

"Let's go to my office," said Lenny.

She pulled Beatrice by the arm, right past Chloe—then past all the pets, and all the pet owners. She escorted her beyond the waiting room, all the way to a quiet corner in the back.

"What happened?" Lenny asked. "I thought you were lying low out there?"

"I was . . ." Beatrice began. She meant to confess every single detail of her encounter with Sam, but standing in front of Lenny, panic set in. "But then I came up with our code names!" she blurted out instead.

"That's the emergency?"

Lenny's shoulders collapsed in relief.

"It could be," said Beatrice. "What if something happens and we're not prepared?"

Some color returned to Lenny's cheeks.

I ALWAYS WANTED A CODE NAME!

"Okay," said Beatrice, rubbing her palms. "You know the phonetic alphabet—how each letter has a name? Like Alpha, Bravo, Charlie, Delta?"

Lenny clapped her hands. "I like the sound of this already."

"I used our initials," Beatrice told her. "Instead of Beatrice Zinker—I'd be Bravo Zulu. Instead of Lenny Santos—you're Lima Sierra!"

Lenny's nose scrunched up.

"No?"

"Not Lima," Lenny said, sticking out her tongue. "I don't want to be a bean."

Beatrice tapped her lip, thinking.

"What if we use Eleanor?" she suggested. "Echo Sierra, undercover?"

Lenny smiled. "I like it!" she said. "What about an emergency phrase?" She glanced around—like Mrs. Tamarack might be lurking nearby—then dropped her voice. "In case we need one . . ."

Beatrice didn't even need to think.

The words rolled off her tongue.

"What about Kinkajou Fever?"

"You yelled Kinkajou Fever, like, three minutes ago, in front of everyone."

"I know," said Beatrice, "but if I ever say it again, you'll know something has gone terribly, terribly wrong."

"Then I hope we never say those words again."

Lenny didn't know it, but it was too late for hoping. Beatrice should have been screaming Kinkajou Fever at the top of her lungs.

As they crossed the playground with the veterinary crowd, Beatrice wished she had confessed to Lenny when she had the chance. Every step closer to the school, her symptoms grew more pronounced.

Guilt ballooned in her chest.

Worry tangled her stomach in knots.

And images of Sam's face throbbed behind her eyes. Like a flickering hologram, she saw the strange new Sam that smiled—then the old shadowy one that fell back into place.

"Are you okay?" asked Lenny. "You look a little funny."

Traffic came to a halt outside the classroom door. Mrs. Tamarack gave a short tweet of her whistle and lifted her hand for attention. "I have a few reminders," she announced. "Please return things to their proper places before you head to the cafeteria.

"If you need a bathroom break, create an orderly line near the coat closet. If you signed up for Foreign Language Club, the first meeting is in the library. Don't forget to bring your lunch."

Mrs. Tamarack swung the door open and the class trampled forward.

Beatrice funneled inside behind Lenny.

Everywhere she looked was a reminder of the disaster with Sam.

Sam's yellow backpack was still missing from its hook in the coat closet. Wes's mail slot was still empty. And Mrs. Tamarack's WANTED poster still screamed at Beatrice from its spot by the pencil sharpener.

Beatrice didn't know where Sam was, but if she blabbed about Beatrice's secret identity, Operation Upside was over.

Beatrice had made a big mistake this morning—and maybe a bigger one with Mrs. Tamarack yesterday—but she wasn't ready to lose their secret operation.

She needed help, and she needed it fast.

Her hand shot up.

"I need to see Ms. Cindy, please!"

Mrs. Tamarack frowned. "Is something wrong?"

"I think I'm sick."

Mrs. Tamarack took one look at Beatrice's pale face and handed her the hall pass. As Beatrice headed out the door, her teacher handed the rest of the class a giant bottle of hand sanitizer.

THREE SQUIRTS FOR EVERYONE, PLEASE!

The apple-scented foam smelled good, but disinfecting was unnecessary. Kinkajou Fever wasn't contagious—it was catastrophic.

13

"You're my favorite patient," said Ms. Cindy, "but we've got to stop meeting like this."

Beatrice collapsed across the counter between them. The smooth surface cooled her hot cheeks.

Ms. Cindy felt her forehead.

"You're not bleeding—that's an improvement! But you do feel a little warm."

"I have Kinkajou Fever," Beatrice confessed.

"Kinkajou Fever, huh? That sounds horrible."

"It is."

Ms. Cindy leaned her elbows on the counter. "Want to tell me about it?"

"Maybe . . ." said Beatrice. Looking into Ms. Cindy's eyes, Beatrice wanted to blurt out all her mistakes. But Operation Upside was a top-secret organization.

This was confidential information. There was only one person she should tell.

Her initials were E.S. And her code name was Echo Sierra.

Ms. Cindy pointed at the chairs in the waiting area. "Why don't you have a seat while you think about it? I'll get you some water— and maybe a snack, since it's almost lunchtime."

Beatrice slumped into one of the seats.

Upside down, some of the pressure emptied out of her head. Her eyelids drifted closed, and her breathing returned to normal.

"Here you go," said Ms. Cindy.

When Beatrice opened her eyes, she barely noticed the water Ms. Cindy offered, or her comforting smile.

All she saw were clunky boots, shuffling past her face.

The boots passed right by Beatrice's head, then trudged out the glass door and into the main corridor of William Charles Elementary.

They weren't just any boots.

These boots belonged to Sam Darzi.

Mr. Hannah, the school counselor, stood in the doorway to his office, waving good-bye. "Stop back anytime, Sam."

"Thanks, Mr. Hannah."

Sam hoisted her bag onto her shoulder and swung around. Her heavy boots carried her away, her yellow backpack drooping behind her.

Halfway down the hall, the bag slid down her sagging shoulders. The zipper gaped open, and something tumbled to the floor.

Beatrice didn't know what Sam lugged around in her yellow bag, but one possibility made her heart pound. Wes's award might be lying in the middle of the hallway.

All she had to do was get up and grab it.

Beatrice flipped out of her seat.

"Thanks, Ms. Cindy!" she yelled on her way out the door. "I'm feeling a lot better now!"

ALWAYS HAPPy to HELP!

14

As Beatrice approached the object, one thing was certain. It was not a piece of paper with Wes Carver's name on it.

Keeping an eye on Sam, Beatrice crouched down to get a better look.

Crumpled on the floor was a tangle of yarn and fabric. Beatrice pinched a corner and lifted it up. Nothing could have surprised her more.

It was a puppet version of Sam.

Beatrice had a similar puppet of her own, fashioned from a forgotten sock she'd found in Mr. Hannah's art supplies. If it were her puppet, she'd want it back.

"Sam!" Beatrice called to the dot drifting down the hall.

Sam did not respond. She continued down the corridor, getting smaller with each step, unaware a piece of her was lying on the floor behind her.

"Sam!" Beatrice yelled again.

Sam kept shrinking farther away.

Beatrice filled up her lungs and shouted once more in her loudest voice. "SAM!!!"

This time Sam turned.

Only half her face was visible in the shadows. The other half was hidden by a veil of hair.

Beatrice held up the puppet.

"You dropped this."

Sam's eye widened. Her hands tightened around the straps of her backpack. Even half-hidden in shadow and hair, the shock on her face was obvious.

Sam opened her mouth like she was about to say something, but before the words reached her lips, she changed her mind and shook her head. "That's not mine," she said instead.

Beatrice stepped closer and slipped the puppet over her hand. "No, see?" She opened and closed the puppet's mouth, mirroring the real Sam. "I saw it fall out of your bag."

Sam's mouth straightened. "I already told you," she repeated, "it's not mine."

The puppet belonged to Sam. The evidence was indisputable.

THE
RESEMBLANCE

THE
EYE WITNESS
REPORT

EXHIBIT
B

REPORT

"I saw
it fall
right out of
her bag."
Beatrice Zinker
WITNESS

But Exhibit C convinced Beatrice to let it go.

EXHIBIT
C

THE SCARY
LOOK ON
SAM'S FACE!

Beatrice pulled the sock off her fingers.
She'd made enough mistakes for one day.

"I'm sorry," she said, staring straight at Sam.
She'd looked so different in the coat closet earlier,
two-eyed and half smiling. Beatrice tucked
the puppet behind her. "My mistake."

"No big deal," said Sam.

She turned her back and
disappeared into the shadows.
Her form grew smaller and
less recognizable with
each step.

With her yellow bag
clutched to her back, she looked
like a deep-sea diver, sinking into
the murky depths of the ocean.

Watching her fade into the
distance, Beatrice felt tethered
to Sam, like they were holding
opposite ends of the same rope.

Today each had kept something that did not belong to them. And neither had said what they were really thinking.

   Beatrice was still trying to make sense of their conversation when the lunch bell rattled above her head.

MAYBE you just NEED SOME FOOD.

15

A stampede of third-graders trampled down the corridor on their way to the cafeteria.

Beatrice flattened herself against the wall, relieved. At least she hadn't missed lunch.

Lenny and Chloe lagged at the end of the pack.

BON APPÉTIT!

Relief spread across Lenny's face when she saw Beatrice. Beatrice stuffed Sam's puppet into her pocket and waved.

"Oh, good—you came back," Lenny said. "Is everything okay?"

"Yeah," said Chloe. "You're acting really weird today."

Lenny tilted her head and studied Beatrice's face. With Chloe around, there was so much they couldn't say.

Beatrice lifted her shoulders. "I'm always weird."

"Weirder than normal," Chloe clarified.

The scent of stuffed-crust pizza filled the air as they reached the end of the hall. "Maybe I'm just hungry," said Beatrice, veering toward the blue doors of the cafeteria.

Chloe stopped. "Aren't you coming to Foreign Language Club?"

Kate's club was the last thing on Beatrice's mind. She looked left and inhaled the promise of comfort food. She glanced to the right, at the wooden doors that led to the library.

Her stomach growled in protest.

Her lunch bag was still sitting in her backpack.

"You can share our lunch," offered Chloe.

Lenny waved a hand in front of Beatrice's face. "You're coming, right?"

Just then, Sam Darzi came around the corner and opened the library doors. Suddenly the decision was easy. The cafeteria had pizza, but the library had Wes's award.

And another chance to get it back.

Beatrice looped her arm through Lenny's. "Of course I'm coming."

Wooden chairs were arranged in four neat rows in the center of the library. Kate stood up front, flipping through flash cards in her red presidential blazer.

Beatrice untangled herself from her friends.

Sam and her yellow backpack were bobbing through books at the back of the room. For the sake of Operation Upside, Beatrice had to try again.

"Save me a seat?" she asked Lenny. "I need to check something out."

"Can't you do it after?"

Beatrice shook her head.

"It might be too late by then."

Chloe wandered up front to introduce herself to Kate.

Lenny narrowed her eyes at Beatrice. "I'm not sure what you're up to, but don't forget—we are lying low, Zulu."

16

Beatrice followed Sam's yellow backpack as it blinked between the stacks. Behind her, Kate was at the podium, already introducing herself to the group. Enthusiastic *bonjour*s and *hola*s rippled through the room.

120

Sam zigged behind
a bookcase.

She zagged around a corner.

With every twist and turn,
Beatrice zigzagged
with her.

Sam finally slowed down in an aisle labeled LANGUAGE. Her fingers scanned the spines as she searched the shelves. At the end of the row, she pulled out a title, then folded to the floor with the book in her lap.

Beatrice scouted for a better view.

400

Sam was studying a
Morse code manual.

Sam's finger followed the alphabet of dots and dashes down the page as Beatrice's heart hammered in her chest. Her mysterious neighbor was up to something.

It looked like Sam had a plan.

One that involved secret code.

A corner of Wes's award peeked out as Sam reached into her backpack. Her hand rummaged past it, digging deeper, and retrieved a long white envelope instead.

A crisp sheet of paper was tucked inside. It wasn't Wes's UPSIDE, but it looked just as official. Without Beatrice's binoculars, though, the lettering was too small to read.

Sam abruptly lifted her nose out of the manual. Looking over both shoulders, she stuffed the letter into the spine and snapped the cover shut.

Sam sulked to the center of the library and slumped into an end seat in the back row of Kate's audience. Beatrice stayed ten steps behind and took the empty seat next to Lenny and Chloe.

"Did I miss anything?" Beatrice asked Lenny.

Chloe put a finger to her lips, then handed Beatrice half a sandwich.

Lenny leaned into Beatrice's ear. "Your sister doesn't mess around. She started at twelve o'clock on the dot." She passed Beatrice a packet of paperwork and a bag of chips. "You already missed the project sign-up."

"Project sign-up?"

In all of Kate's practice sessions, Beatrice had never heard about a project. She crunched a chip in frustration.

First no stuffed-crust pizza.

Now homework?

"Chloe and I already partnered up." Lenny grimaced an apology. "You can only have two people per group."

FOREIGN LANGUAGE
CLUB
GROUP PROJECT #1
DUE: NEXT TUESDAY
☑ CHOOSE A GROUP
☑ CHOOSE A LANGUAGE

Kate stopped midsentence at the front of the room. Her eyes zeroed in on Beatrice. "It looks like we have a latecomer."

Kate's presentation froze on the screen behind her.

"Hi," said Beatrice, with a little wave.

"Bonjour," said Kate, in her trying-to-be-patient voice. "We've already divided into groups of two for the project. Do you want to be with Lenny?"

Lenny nodded vigorously, encouraging Beatrice to say yes.

"I could make an exception for you," Kate said.

Beatrice hesitated.

She wanted to work with Lenny, but her eyes drifted to the back row where Sam was slouched in her seat, flipping pages in her Morse code manual.

"Actually," said Beatrice, looking up at Kate, "I have a different idea."

Panic flushed across her sister's face. "A different idea?"

"If it's okay with you," said Beatrice, "I want to work on a special project with Sam Darzi."

Lenny's mouth dropped open.

Sound disappeared from the already quiet library. Heads ping-ponged around the room, bouncing between Beatrice and Kate and the dark-haired girl in the back row.

Sam's eyes were fixed on her boots.

Kate gripped the podium.

"What do you have in mind?" she asked.

"A special project," said Beatrice. "About secret languages."

"Like Pig Latin?"

"Pig Latin, and other things…" Beatrice peeked back at Sam. "Like Morse code."

Sam flipped her book facedown and looked away with a frown.

Kate tilted her head, considering.

A roomful of heads tilted with her.

"*Très bien,*" she finally declared. "I like it."

She passed Beatrice the sign-up sheet.

Whispers replaced the silence, as opinions spattered through the room.

Chloe leaned over. "See what I mean about being weird?"

Lenny bit into her sandwich, waiting to see what Beatrice would say.

Beatrice shrugged. "It's a weird day."

Having a secret from Lenny was the weirdest thing in the world. She wished Lenny already knew about Sam—what Sam saw, what she knew, and most of all, what she was carrying in her backpack.

Even more than that, Beatrice wished she could undo her mistake. Maybe there was still a way to fix it before Lenny found out.

Beatrice added Sam's name next to her own, then passed the clipboard back to Kate.

"Merci," she mouthed in her sister's favorite language.

Kate nodded. "Next time, don't be late."

Beatrice glanced at the back row—to the reason for her tardiness—but Sam was gone.

17

After dinner, Beatrice escaped to her room to think. She hauled her backpack onto the top bunk and removed Sam's puppet.

The puppet's one eye watched Beatrice warily as she arranged the strands on Sam's head. The button never blinked. Beatrice gazed back, wishing she could figure out the mystery of Sam Darzi if she stared hard enough, or looked long enough.

Beatrice fitted the puppet over her hand. The puppet continued to observe her with its one oversized eye.

Beatrice lifted the yarn off the puppet's forehead. The curiosity was impossible to resist. To her surprise, another eye peeked out.

"Wow," said Beatrice. "Sam actually gave you two eyes."

It was a promising sign.

"There's someone I want you to meet," she told the sock on her hand.

"Sam, this is Beatrice," she said, introducing a puppet version of herself to Sam's sock. "Beatrice, this is Sam."

Beatrice flipped upside down and all three heads hung off the bunk.

"Whoa," said Sam's puppet.

"I know," said Beatrice. "It's the best."

"Now I have a headache," the sock complained.

"That's what Kate always says," said Beatrice. She stared at Sam's sock. Upside down, it looked completely different. "But I like the view."

Sam's puppet frowned.

Upside down it looked a lot like a smile.

The almost-smile gave Beatrice the courage to ask the one thing she'd always wanted to know about Sam.

"Why don't you talk to anyone?"

Sam's sock didn't answer right away.

Eventually, it mumbled, "Maybe I don't have anything to say."

Beatrice didn't believe that. Not for a second.

"Everyone has something to say." She opened her hand and moved Sam's puppet mouth.

Hi! MY NAME is SAM AND I HAVE SO MUCH to SAY....

"Are you talking to yourself?"

Kate stood in the doorway, smirking.

Beatrice shoved the puppets behind her back. "I'm just doing some research. For my project."

Kate leaned against the bunk. "So," she said. "What's it like working with Sam so far?"

There was only one word for it.

"Mysterious," said Beatrice. "Very mysterious."

As Kate wandered into their closet to hang up her blazer, Beatrice had an idea.

"Hey, Kate? Can I borrow your cape?"

Her sister's sigh drifted across the room.

"It's a *pon-cho*." Kate drew out the word, like its two syllables were each a mile long, and then marched to the bed, cape in hand.

"Here," she said, draping the fabric over Beatrice's bedpost. "Just keep it."

"Really?" said Beatrice. "Thanks! It's going to be perfect for tomorrow!"

Beatrice lifted up the blinds and smiled out into the night.

Wes would still get his award.

She was going to turn this disaster around.

Sam Darzi lived right across the street. They sat in Classroom 3B together five days a week. They were working on a special project—and now Beatrice owned a cape.

Sam couldn't stay a mystery forever.

18

The next morning, fog gave way to sunshine.

    In the early yellow light, the world looked fresh and full of potential. Each blade of grass sparkled, and the changing trees showed off their colors.

    Beatrice couldn't wait to talk to Sam.

While the rest of
the sidewalk glittered
in sunlight, the Darzi
house still looked
gloomy. Shades
cloaked the windows.
The overgrown tree
in the front yard
swallowed the porch
in shadow.

Sam's house looked
a lot like Sam.

"Good morning, dear!" called a friendly voice behind Beatrice. A red leash curled around her legs, and Scrappy's familiar face mewed up at her.

Beatrice spun around in surprise.

"Mrs. Jenkins!" she cried.

"Have you seen Sam this morning?" Mrs. Jenkins lifted a book with a fancy yellow bow tied around it. "I want to thank her for taking care of Scrappy while I was away."

Beatrice shook her head back and forth.

She hadn't seen Sam yet.

"That's okay," said Mrs. Jenkins, patting her hand. "I'll see her this afternoon."

"Sam was helping you?"

"Wasn't that nice of her?" Mrs. Jenkins's face tilted up at the sky. Her silver hair glowed in the sunshine. "Isn't it a beautiful day?"

She untangled the leash from Beatrice's legs and scooped Scrappy into her arms. "Don't forget to come see us later. As usual—we'll have tea!"

Mrs. Jenkins waved and continued down the road, Scrappy tucked under one arm and Sam's present under the other.

As they turned the corner, Beatrice studied Sam's window. She wondered again what Sam planned to do with Wes's award.

There were a lot of possibilities.

Some prospects were bad—but there were some good ones too.

REPORT BEATRICE to MR. HANNAH

TURN OVER THE EVIDENCE to MRS. TAMARACK

DESTROY THE EVIDENCE

RETURN THE AWARD to BEATRICE

GIVE THE UPSIDE DIRECTLY to WES

It was a beautiful day, just like Mrs. Jenkins had said, so Beatrice flipped her cape over her shoulder, hopped on the bus, and hoped for the best.

When Beatrice arrived at school, everything seemed normal.

Wes was greeting students at the front door, just like he always did. He wasn't smiling like someone who had just received an award with his name lettered in gold.

When Mr. Hannah passed Beatrice in the hall, he didn't give her a second glance. Apparently, Sam hadn't ratted Beatrice out in the counselor's office yesterday, either.

Beatrice walked into Classroom 3B and found Lenny and Chloe huddled together with the rest of the veterinary crew, trying on lab coats and using Lenny's new stencils.

In the corner by the pencil sharpener, Mrs. Tamarack's WANTED poster still urged witnesses to come forward.

As the bell rang, Mrs. Tamarack clapped her hands and flicked the lights.

Sam Darzi snuck in the door right before Mrs. Tamarack clicked it shut. With her head down, she shuffled straight to the coat closet.

"Hi!" Beatrice said, trying to get her attention.

Sam acted like she didn't see her.

But Beatrice knew she did.

After talking to Sam's puppet last night, Beatrice had high hopes. But Sam walked away without a word. Beatrice didn't even get to tell her about Mrs. Jenkins.

Watching Sam's boots scuff across the floor brought Beatrice back to reality. The real Sam hadn't had a heart-to-heart with her last night.

The real Sam was not a puppet.

She was a person, and Beatrice couldn't make her say a thing. She couldn't even make her stand still long enough to say *hello*.

As Beatrice headed back to her desk, Lenny pointed at Beatrice's cape, frowning. "I thought you had enough pink to last forever?"

Mrs. Tamarack clapped her hands at the front of the room.

"Recess?" mouthed Beatrice.

Lenny nodded.

"One, two, three—eyes on me!" Mrs. Tamarack called out, shooting them a look.

Beatrice took a deep, hopeful breath.

Nothing was different.

Wes was the same. Mr. Hannah was acting normal. Sam and Lenny too. Even Mrs. Tamarack seemed like her normal self.

Whatever Sam was going to do with the award, she hadn't done it yet.

19

When recess arrived, Beatrice was the first one out the door. She inched into the trees and rehearsed her confession to Lenny.

Down below, something stopped Beatrice in her tracks.

Mrs. Tamarack stood guard at the center of the playground—hands on her hips, whistle between her lips.

That part was normal.

Beatrice was used to that.

Standing next to the school's award-winning disciplinarian, rocking back and forth on the heels of her boots, was Sam Darzi.

This was cause for alarm.

Beatrice couldn't hear what they were saying, but it didn't look good. Mrs. Tamarack's forehead was scrunched up, and Sam—who rarely spoke—was doing most of the talking.

Finally, with a nod of her head, Sam disappeared across the grass and behind the heavy doors of William Charles Elementary.

Sam was making her move.

Beatrice needed to stop her before it was too late. Thinking fast, she dropped down near Mrs. Tamarack and made a move of her own.

"Excuse me," said Beatrice, summoning her best manners.

Mrs. Tamarack spun around. Her whistle shrilled in surprise. "Beatrice!" she screamed. "Are you trying to give me a heart attack?"

"No! I was trying to be polite."

Mrs. Tamarack rubbed her temples.

"May I go inside with Sam, please?" Beatrice asked, still using her best manners. "We're partners on a project," she explained, hoping Mrs. Tamarack would give away Sam's destination.

"Fine," Mrs. Tamarack conceded. "I just sent her to the library."

"The library?" Beatrice couldn't keep the surprise out of her voice. She was expecting the office, or the classroom. Not the library.

Unless the library was Sam's cover story . . .

"Of course, the library," said Mrs. Tamarack. She took the whistle out of her mouth and pointed it at Beatrice. "Keep an eye on the time—and your feet on the ground. The library is not a playground."

After checking the coat closet in Classroom 3B, and peeking in the doorway to Mr. Hannah's office—just in case—Beatrice found Sam nestled in a beanbag chair at the back of the library.

The Morse code manual lay open on her lap.

She frowned as Beatrice approached.

Beatrice plopped down beside her. "I thought we could work on our project."

"I never said I wanted to do that project."

"There's only one Morse code book in the library. It makes sense to share it."

Sam snapped the book shut.

"Here," she said, sliding the book across the table between them. "You keep it."

Beatrice fitted her fingers into Sam's puppet and pulled it from the pocket of her cape. "What about a different trade?" she proposed. "I'll give you your puppet back, and you give me Wes's award?"

Sam stared her down.

OR NOT.

Instead of responding to Beatrice's offer, Sam smirked. "I can't believe you wrote 'Most Strict' on Mrs. Tamarack's award. . . ."

Beatrice slumped in her seat. "It was supposed to be a compliment!"

Sam raised her eyebrows. Her smirk deepened.

This was not going well.

Leaning forward, Beatrice asked Sam the question that had haunted her since yesterday. "What are you going to do with Wes's award?"

A bit of desperation tinged her voice.

And her question came out as a demand.

Sam crossed her arms and raised her chin. "I don't know yet," she said. Then, seizing her bag, she pushed herself out of the oversized cushion.

This time, as Sam disappeared, she wasn't a deep-sea diver slipping into nothingness. She didn't shuffle out of sight. She stood a little straighter than normal, and stalked away with the confidence of a special agent.

Beatrice studied the puppet in her hand.

Under all the tangled yarn, Sam had two eyes and a smile. Beatrice leaned back and opened Sam's book, pondering.

Pieces of a plan flipped over in her mind as she leafed through the pages. She couldn't see the full puzzle yet, but she saw enough to press forward.

The first step was finding her partner in crime.

Before Beatrice did anything else, Lenny deserved the truth.

20

TRUTH BE TOLD

Beatrice didn't have to wait long to talk to Lenny.

Moments later, an opportunity crashed through the library doors.

"I've been looking everywhere for you!" said Lenny.

Her hair was disheveled, and her bangs were stuck to her forehead.

"What's going on?" asked Beatrice.

"I can't stand looking at his sad face one more second." Lenny held up a finger. Her body bent over as she huffed and puffed and tried to catch her breath.

Beatrice didn't need to ask who Lenny was talking about.

It had to be Wes.

A smattering of kids dotted the tables around them. Too many of them were peeking in their direction.

"Come on," said Beatrice, grabbing Lenny's arm and heading for the exit. "We need privacy."

Once the wooden doors thudded behind them, Lenny's words tumbled out in a rush. "Did you know Chloe put up that 'Girls Only' sign just to keep Wes out? I just asked her to take it down, but it takes a long time to change Chloe's mind."

Lenny paused and took a shaky breath.

"I know there's still a 'Wanted' poster, and I know it's a really big risk, but I think we need to give Wes his award today." Her earnest eyes peered into Beatrice's face. "It's still in your backpack, right?"

Beatrice swallowed.

". . . I have Kinkajou Fever."

The admission came out in a mumble.

Lenny stared at her blankly, so Beatrice said their emergency phrase again.

This time louder.

"I have Kinkajou Fever!" she half shouted.

"I need you to be serious, Beatrice."

"I *am* being serious."

"Wait—" Lenny's voice rose as the emergency phrase sank in. "You have Kinkajou Fever?!"

Beatrice nodded.

"If you think Wes's face was sad today, you should have seen his face when Chloe first put up that 'No Boys Allowed' sign."

Her eyes met Lenny's.

"I *had* to give him the award," Beatrice explained.

"He has it?" said Lenny. A breath of relief puffed out of her cheeks. "Wes already has his award?"

Beatrice stared at the floor.

"Actually . . ." she admitted, "Sam Darzi has it."

Lenny threw her hands in the air.

"How is that even possible?"

"I accidently put Wes's award into Sam's mailbox," said Beatrice, grimacing.

Lenny looked even more confused.

"I was upside down," Beatrice told her. "And Sam's name looked a lot like *Wes*."

Lenny's mouth dropped open. "Sam didn't see you, did she?"

"She definitely saw me," said Beatrice. "Upside down and everything."

"This is really bad, Beatrice."

"The way I see it, we have two options." Beatrice held up two fingers. "First, there's Plan A." She dropped one finger down. "We cut our losses and make a brand-new award for Wes."

"Okay," said Lenny. She chewed her thumbnail. "That can work."

"Plan A has some downsides, though," Beatrice warned. "If we don't get Wes's original UPSIDE back, Sam has a lot of evidence against us. Especially since she saw me delivering it." She lifted her hand in apology. "And your stencils are all over it."

Lenny clunked her head against the wall.

"Plan B better be good, Beatrice."

"It is," Beatrice said. "All we need to do is make sure Wes gets the original award."

Lenny lifted her head. "How do we do that?"

This was the one piece of the puzzle Beatrice knew.

"We need Sam's help."

"Sam doesn't even talk to us—why would she help?" Lenny slid down the wall and plopped to the ground. "We are so doomed."

"I don't think so," said Beatrice. As the words came out, her confidence grew. "I think we have a chance."

REALLY?

"Plan B's going to work," Beatrice declared. "I'm almost sure of it."

She helped Lenny to her feet as the bell chirped noon.

"Come on," said Beatrice. "We can figure out the details while we eat."

The cofounders of Operation Upside strode toward the cafeteria with Beatrice's cape billowing behind them.

Flying high was so much easier than lying low.

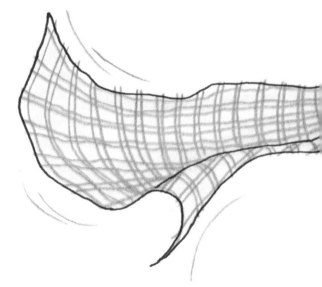

21

Wednesday was beefy nachos day in the cafeteria.

Nothing compared to stuffed-crust pizza, but nachos were still good news.

The nachos came with cheese, salsa, and a big scoop of meat in a styrofoam cup, which completely grossed Chloe out. While Chloe bit into homemade peanut-butter-and-jelly, Lenny and Beatrice stood in the lunch line, brainstorming Plan B.

"Do you think Sam would make a trade?" asked Lenny.

Beatrice shook her head. "Already tried that."

"Oh," said Lenny. Her face dropped. "Then what's the plan?"

She stepped forward and grabbed two empty trays from the rack.

Beatrice didn't answer Lenny right away.

Her concentration was elsewhere.

Wes Carver was meandering through the maze of cafeteria tables. Instead of looking for rocks, he was searching for a seat.

Lenny passed Beatrice a tray.

Beatrice accepted it absently.

"Let's invite Sam to join Operation Upside," said Beatrice. She slid her tray next to Lenny's. "Everyone wants to be included, right?"

Uncertainty clouded Lenny's face.

"Can we trust her?"

Beatrice passed Lenny a boat of nachos.

She spied Sam in the far corner of the cafeteria, at a table dominated by fourth-grade boys. As usual, their heads were clustered over their trading cards. Sam sat two seats over, her feet propped on the table, her face masked in a book.

As if sensing Beatrice's attention, Sam's gaze flicked up. Still pretending to read, she eyed Beatrice through her dark shroud of hair.

Beatrice picked up a cup of ground beef and a container of cheese. "I hope so," she told Lenny. "She'd be a great spy."

Lenny regarded Sam with a slight smile.

"That's definitely true."

"So," Beatrice asked. "What should we do?"

Lenny carried her tray to the cashier.

Consideration lined her face as they checked out.

"This is going to take some work," she said. "When we ask her, we need to get it exactly right."

Beatrice and Lenny utilized every spare moment of the afternoon to perfect their plan.

During silent reading, Beatrice buried her nose in Morse code while Lenny mapped out every possible scenario in her journal.

During Science, they weighed their options,

then used Social Studies to vote on a winner. During Math, they broke down the plan and divided it into three parts.

Phase I
The Planning
Phase II
The Preparation
Phase III
The Proposal!

By the time the bell rang, Phase I was complete.

At the buses, they parted ways. From that moment forward, Beatrice would be on her own.

Lenny cleared her throat. "Call me when you get to the safe house," she said. "We can practice your lines one more time. Then I'll cross my fingers until I fall asleep."

Beatrice nodded gratefully.

Echo Sierra had her back—even if she couldn't follow her home.

It was the second-longest bus ride of the week.

Every second Beatrice spent on the bus was one less moment she could spend preparing for tonight.

When Mr. Madeline, the bus driver, opened the door on her street, Beatrice darted past her sister—and her sister's friends—and hurried down the block, with only a quick wave to Mrs. Jenkins as she sped by.

Beatrice raced up the Zinkers' porch and plowed through the front door. After pausing to greet Henry, she grabbed the phone from the kitchen counter and sprinted upstairs to make contact.

"I made it to the safe house," she said, out of breath, when Lenny answered.

"Okay," said Lenny, crunching what sounded like a carrot. "Let's start with Scenario #1, then try Scenario #2. I'll be Sam. And you be you."

Together they rehearsed Beatrice's lines over and over, until she was more than ready. Lenny wished Beatrice good luck; then they hung up so Beatrice could prepare the supplies.

After gathering everything on the list, she spent the next half hour memorizing Morse patterns, writing top-secret instructions, and perfecting her escape route.

Exhausted, she collapsed on her bed.

Phase II was done, but the hardest part was still ahead.

Everything hinged on Phase III.

The final piece of the plan required patience, careful timing, and a little luck. Beatrice watched for a window of opportunity when no one would notice her missing. All evening she was on high alert, watching for a moment of peak distraction.

NOT YET

CAN YOU CHANGE HENRY? I THINK HE'S WET....

IF ONLY

SPELL LONELY....

Her chance came halfway through dinner when Henry picked up his plastic utensils and started a drum solo.

A few minutes into Henry's performance, Beatrice paused with her fork halfway to her mouth. Her eyes roamed the table to see if anyone else heard what she was hearing.

Henry's drumsticks were banging out a pattern.

Rat-a-rat-a-tat. Rat-a-rat-a-rat. Rat-a-tat. Rat-a-rat-a-rat. Tat-a-rat-a-rat.

Beatrice stole a glance at her brother. He looked like an innocent baby, but she knew better. Henry was playing more than rhythm.

He was playing letters.

The same exact letters, over and over again.

G-O-N-O-W-G-O-N-O-W

Henry raised his spoons above his head and brought them down with a crash. Then, in perfect Morse rhythm, he spelled it out again.

Rat-a-rat-a-tat.

Rat-a-rat-a-rat.

Rat-a-tat.

Rat-a-rat-a-rat.

Tat-a-rat-a-rat.

G O   N O W!

All her doubts disintegrated.

Henry meant the message for her.

This was her moment.

Beatrice balanced her fork on the edge of her plate and downed the rest of her water. It was important to hydrate before a mission.

"Pete?" said Nancy Zinker. "Do you think Henry's too young for music lessons?"

"Not when he's got rhythm like that." Pete Zinker reached into the drawer behind him for a pair of pencils and joined the noise. "The Zinkers are in the house!"

Nancy Zinker rushed for the video camera.

Henry was right.

Her window was officially open.

"May I be excused?" Beatrice asked.

Her dad didn't hear the question over the beat of his drumsticks.

Her mother peered above the video camera. "Can you take some photos while I record this?"

"I will!" Kate chirped.

Beatrice raised her eyebrows in surprise.

First Henry. Now Kate.

More than luck was on her side tonight.

Upstairs, Beatrice suited up.

Phase III required the deluxe ninja suit.

THINKING CAP

MASK

BACKPACK

GLOVES

WINDOW OF OPPORTUNITY

CAPE

Slinging her backpack over her shoulder, Beatrice stepped through the window of opportunity and onto the roof. With a little wish and a lot of hope, she took a running leap and jumped into the mystery of Plan B.

22

It only took four moves to get from
her roof to Sam's.

THE
RUNNING
LEAP

THE
LOOK BOTH
WAYS!

THE
CAT
BURGLAR

THE
JUST-FOR-
FUN

Up close, Sam's window looked the same as it did from a distance.

All closed up.

The blinds were drawn. The light was off.

Beatrice crouched down and dug into her pack. Her flashlight was at the very bottom.

With her eyes shut and her finger on the switch, she pressed the lens to the glass and concentrated on the patterns she'd practiced all afternoon.

Three short flicks of light for *S*.

Flick, flick, flick.

She counted to three, then moved to the next letter.

A was one quick flick, followed by one long flash.

Flick, flash.

Her heart pounded out three more beats.

Then two long flashes for the *M*.

Flash, flash.

She rested the flashlight in her lap and counted ten Mississippis. Then she lifted her flashlight and repeated the patterns.

Flick, flick, flick.

Pause.

Flick, flash.

Pause.

Flash, flash.

Pause.

S. Pause. *A.* Pause. *M.* Pause.

Slowly and carefully, ten times in a row, Beatrice spelled out Sam's name in light.

On her eleventh *S*, the blinds slid up.

On the eleventh *A*, the window lifted.

On the eleventh *M*, Sam stuck out her head.

Her arm
blocked the beam
of light shining
at her face.

"Turn that thing off,"
she said. "We do have a door, you know."

Beatrice shrugged. "This seemed easier."

Sam glanced through the open window, back into her house. The corner of her mouth lifted. "You might be right."

She ducked inside her room.

When she reappeared, she was zipping a sweatshirt and pulling up the hood. "I've never been on the roof," she admitted as she climbed over the windowsill.

Neither spoke for a few seconds.

Staring at Sam's boots, Beatrice forgot all her well-rehearsed lines. Hopefully Lenny remembered to keep her fingers crossed.

Sam broke the silence first.

"Nice cape."

"Thanks," said Beatrice. "It's my sister's." She pointed at Sam's feet. "I like your boots."

"They're my brother's," said Sam.

"You have a brother?"

"I just said I did," Sam snapped. Her face dared Beatrice to ask again.

Beatrice had never seen Sam's brother—a mom and a grandmother, but not a brother.

Sam blew a lock of hair out of her face. "Is there a reason you're on my roof in that outfit?"

All of Beatrice's practiced dialogue came rushing back. She swung her backpack around and announced, "I have a delivery for you."

"I don't want one of your awards, Beatrice."

"It's not an award."

Beatrice pulled Sam's puppet from a zippered pocket and held it out to her.

"Here," she offered.

"I already told you," said Sam. "It's not mine."

Beatrice ignored her and said the words she came to say. "Inside the puppet you will find your mission, should you choose to accept it."

Sam pushed her hair behind her ear. "You're really into this spy thing, huh?"

Beatrice lifted her flashlight and flooded Sam's face with light. "Are you in, or are you out?"

Sam squinted against the brightness.

"Seriously," she said. "Turn that thing off."

She shoved the flashlight out of her face.

Then she bent over her boots and fixed her laces. Upside down, she said, "If I were interested— and I'm not saying I am—how would I let you know?"

Beatrice held in a smile.

She slipped Sam's puppet over her fingers.

Sam yanked the sock from Beatrice's hand. Her fingers fished out a note, then stuffed the puppet into her sweatshirt pocket.

Beatrice watched Sam's eyes trace the words she'd written earlier. At the bottom of the page, she didn't look up. Instead, Sam rubbed a spot on her boot and asked, "How long do I have to decide?"

This was going better than Beatrice anticipated. "As long as you want?"

Sam pointed at her accusingly. "Do not smile about this," she warned. "I'm not making any promises."

"That's okay," said Beatrice. "I never make promises either."

Beatrice wished Sam a good night, then hurried back to her bedroom window before anyone noticed her missing.

When her mom tucked her in and twisted the blinds for the night, Sam's blinds were still open, and her light was still on. It looked like the house across the street had finally come to life.

Plan B had no guarantees, but Beatrice went to sleep smiling.

23
SAM'S ANSWER

Thursday came and went without word from Sam.

Whenever Beatrice tried to make eye contact in class, Sam looked away.

"Did you give her a deadline?" Lenny asked.

"Not really," said Beatrice. "It was kind of open-ended."

Lenny bit her thumbnail. "How long are we going to wait?"

"As long as it takes."

"Wow," said Lenny.

Beatrice shrugged.

"I have a good feeling about this."

Sam's answer came Friday night, just before bedtime. It was Kate who sounded the alarm.

"Beatrice!" she yelled down the stairs. "You need to come up here!"

Beatrice bounded up the steps, traveling so fast she tripped twice before reaching their room.

Her sister was at the window, peeking through the blinds. "There's a light show going on across the street," said Kate. "I have a feeling it has something to do with you."

Beatrice leaned over Kate's shoulder.

Sure enough, a beam of light flashed across the street. On and off it pulsed, lighting up the night.

After forty-eight hours of silence, Sam was finally talking.

Light flicked and flashed across the space between them like a song. Beatrice blinked her eyes, mesmerized by the beauty of it.

Flick.

Flick, flick, flick.

Flash, flick, flash, flash.

Flick, flash.

Flash, flick, flash, flash.

Beatrice watched as the letters cycled over and over, trying to make sense of them. They weren't the letters she was expecting. Sam was supposed to signal her choice. IN or OUT.

But Sam was saying something else.

"Are you practicing for your project?" Kate wanted to know.

"Hold on," Beatrice said, squinting. "I need to concentrate."

Beatrice grabbed her binoculars and focused on the blinking window. She translated dots and dashes for all the flicks and flashes.

Flick was E.

Flick, flick, flick was S.

Flash, flick, flash, flash was Y.

Flick, flash was A.

Flash, flick, flash, flash was another *Y*.

E-S-Y-A-Y

When Beatrice figured it out, her binoculars dropped to the floor. Sam was using Morse code to tell her YES in Pig Latin.

"Why are you smiling like that?" Kate waved a hand in front of Beatrice's face. "Are you okay?"

Beatrice nodded her head and swallowed the lump in her throat. *"Es-yay,"* she told Kate. "I'm just really happy."

For once, she understood Sam perfectly.

24

Monday morning started like it always did.

Sam slipped into Classroom 3B just as the bell rang. As usual, she ignored Beatrice's attempts at *hello*.

"Are you sure she was saying yes?" Lenny said.

"I'm positive," said Beatrice.

Deep down, though, she was wondering the same thing, and by lunchtime, doubt had swallowed her appetite completely.

"If you don't want your apple, I'll take it," offered Chloe. "Mine's mushy."

Beatrice handed it over, then passed Lenny her cookie. Across the cafeteria, Sam's face was deep in her book.

She never even glanced in their direction.

At the very end of the day, Beatrice found a note stuffed in her mailbox. Her gasp of relief almost blew her cover.

Mrs. Tamarack looked over, scowling. "Nose to sleeve when you sneeze, Beatrice!"

She lifted an elbow to her face in demonstration.

Beatrice stuffed the note into her pocket and smiled. "Got it!"

As the whole school flooded to the buses, Beatrice and Lenny dove for the bushes. They only had a few minutes to spare.

Beatrice quickly decoded the dots, dashes, and slashes while Lenny rushed to scribble them down.

TUESDAY /
0845 / HOURS /
WAiT / iN / YOUR /
FAVOriTE /
TREE / BY /
THE / DOOR /
S

Lenny stuck her pencil in her hair.

"I like her already," she declared.

A satisfied smile spread across Beatrice's face. "I know," she said. "She's a natural."

At precisely 8:45 a.m. the next morning, concealed in the leafy cover of the designated tree, Beatrice and Lenny pulled out their binoculars and zoomed in on the front doors of William Charles Elementary.

Lenny spotted it first.

"Look!" she whispered, pointing. "Right by the planter."

Seeing what Sam had done, Beatrice's chest hurt. A part of her wished they'd planned to give Sam the UPSIDE all along.

She deserved it as much as anyone.

Sam's house, blinds-up and bright, flashed through Beatrice's mind. Maybe being included was as good as getting an award anyway.

Maybe it was even better.

"Do you think it's safe down there?" Lenny pulled her binoculars from her face. "What if Wes is late and someone else finds it first?"

Questions were still coming out of Lenny's mouth when Wes Carver wandered into view.

The package immediately caught his attention. Squatting down, he retrieved the award.

Confusion flickered across his features for a moment. Then he spun in a full circle, looking all around, happiness beaming from every part of his face.

"We don't even need binoculars to see that smile," said Beatrice.

"What are you guys doing up there?"

Chloe Llewelyn stood below them with a giant poster rolled under her arm. "You're not being another weird animal, are you? I don't have time to make new rules all day."

"Hey, Chloe," said Lenny. "You know what you need?" She stashed the binoculars and adjusted her position. "An assistant who can keep up with all Beatrice's animals."

Lenny nodded toward the front door.

"Like *him*."

Chloe angled her head and studied Wes. He held his new award in one hand and the front door in the other.

His eyes were shining, and his morning greetings were more enthusiastic than ever. . . .

But his T-shirt said it best.

Chloe pursed her lips, considering.

"Maybe . . ." she finally said. "He does know a lot about animals. And did you know his pink marker smells *exactly* like watermelon?"

Beatrice and Lenny exchanged a smile.

From Chloe, a *maybe* was a very good sign.

Three hours later, Sam slipped into the library and took a seat next to Beatrice. "I can't believe I'm doing this," she whispered.

Lenny and Chloe were in the middle of an impressive presentation about the Philippines. Chloe colored a detailed map, and Lenny showed a bunch of photos from her summer vacation.

They even taught everyone how to say *hello* and introduce themselves in Tagalog.

The best part was the banana-cue.

Lenny's mom made a whole platter of the Filipino treat. It looked like barbecued chicken on a stick, but it was really a fried banana with a sticky sugar coating.

Beatrice raised her hand. "How do you say *delicious* in Tagalog?"

so GOOD!

"*Masarap!*" said Lenny.

Everyone agreed. Banana-cue was very *masarap*.

Lenny and Chloe weren't the only pair to bring snacks. Trying new food was so fun, Beatrice almost forgot she was missing another pizza day in the cafeteria.

After all the other presentations were finished, Beatrice and Sam walked up to the podium with their puppets tucked in their pockets.

It was time for their special project.

"We need just a minute to get ready," Beatrice told the room.

Together they flipped the presentation table on its side and took their places behind their stage. Beatrice lifted her puppet above her head and began the show.

LIKE MANY OF you — I WASN'T SURE I WANTED to JOIN tHIS CLUB....

In the front row, Kate cleared her throat.

Sam jumped in to help.

BUt — LIKE MANY OF YOU — WE'RE GLAD WE DiD!

Beatrice picked it back up again.

"Languages can be really confusing. Sometimes you have no idea what someone is saying. Or you think someone is saying one thing, but they're actually saying something else."

Kate cleared her throat again.

"Last week, Sam and I didn't understand each other at all," Beatrice continued. "Now I know some Morse code, and Sam knows some Pig Latin."

For a moment, all the faces in the library faded away. All Beatrice saw was Sam's window, flickering with light, saying YES in both their languages.

Behind the table, Beatrice smiled at Sam.

Sam smiled right back.

"And it turns out," Sam's puppet told the crowd, "we both speak Puppet."

After that, the presentation was a blur.

Beatrice forgot to mention all the cool facts she'd memorized about Morse code, or why she loved Pig Latin so much. No one seemed to notice. When she and Sam bowed at the end, the entire room was laughing and clapping—including Kate.

Best of all, Sam was smiling with her whole face, in front of everyone.

While they packed up, Beatrice passed Sam a folded scrap of paper. Sam opened the note and scanned the invitation.

FRIDAY.
YOUR ROOF.
1900 HOURS
SHARP!

Without glancing at Beatrice, Sam creased the message closed. Her fingers continued working, pleating the paper into a gum-sized rectangle. She folded the top-secret information into her cheek and began to chew.

Beatrice lifted her eyebrows.

That was one way to hide confidential information.

Beatrice couldn't wait to tell Lenny.

"Save room for dessert," she told Sam. "The password is *ice cream*."

Sam remained silent, but the corner of her mouth quirked up. Her jaw was still hard at work, destroying their secret communication. With a little wave, she headed into the hall, her eyes gleaming and her mouth full of secrets.

Most things about Sam remained a mystery, but one thing was certain. Sam Darzi was meant for Operation Upside.

25

Friday night, when all three girls had whispered the password and settled onto Sam's roof, Beatrice brought the meeting to order.

WHEN I CALL YOUR NAME, PLEASE SAY "HERE."

Sam looked at Lenny. "Is she always like this?"

"Pretty much," Lenny laughed.

Beatrice's puppet called out the first name. "Echo Sierra?"

"Here!" said Lenny.

"Sierra Delta?"

"Here," Sam muttered.

"Bravo Zulu?" the sock called out.

"Here!" Beatrice confirmed.

Lenny pointed to three bowls perched on the windowsill. "Now that we're all here, can we eat the ice cream?"

"Good idea," said Beatrice. "Before it gets too melty."

Lenny doled out the ice cream while Beatrice passed out spoons.

Sam balanced her bowl on her knee. "If it's okay," she started, bouncing her boots nervously, "there's something I want to say." She reached through her bedroom window and grabbed her yellow backpack.

Beatrice and Lenny waited, their full attention on Sam as she unzipped the bag.

"My brother's in the navy," she confided. "He writes me a lot of letters." She held up a handful of worn envelopes. "They're always in code."

She paused and pushed her hair behind her ear.

"Last week, he sent one in Morse."

"Oh . . ." said Beatrice. The library envelope was from Sam's brother. "That's why you checked out the Morse code book?"

Sam nodded.

"Learning Morse was more fun than I expected—but naval flags are my favorite secret language."

Her arm slipped into her backpack.

She lifted up a tiny paper flag wrapped around a toothpick and waved it back and forth.

"There's one flag for every letter of the alphabet. They all mean something specific."

Beatrice touched the blue-and-yellow patch sewn onto Sam's backpack. "Is that one?"

"That's K." Sam smiled. "KILO."

"What's it mean?" asked Lenny, leaning forward for a better look.

"It means *I wish to communicate with you.*" Sam stared at the envelopes in her lap. "My brother sent it in his first letter."

Her hand disappeared into her bag again. "Here—I made some for you."

She lifted a red-and-white flag in her right hand. "This one's BRAVO." She raised a multi-colored flag in her left. "And this one's ZULU."

Sam leaned over and stuck two flags into Beatrice's ice cream. Then she did the same for Lenny.

Beatrice and Lenny looked down at their ice cream, then back at Sam, waiting for a translation.

"You guys really don't know what BRAVO ZULU means?"

"It's Beatrice's code name," said Lenny. "That's all I know."

Sam checked with Beatrice. "You don't know either?"

Beatrice shook her head.

"I can't believe I get to be the one to tell you."

Clearing her throat, Sam lifted a miniature version of each flag. "Flown together these flags are a celebration," she explained, wiggling the toothpicks. "BRAVO ZULU means *well done.*"

Beatrice stared at Sam with her mouth open. "Is that true?"

Sam held out a book from her bag. A grid of flags decorated the cover. "You can look it up later."

Beatrice took the book. She'd seen it once before—in Mrs. Jenkins's hands, topped with a yellow bow.

Lenny bumped her shoulder.

"Bravo Zulu, Beatrice," she said. "I don't know how you did it. You recruited Sam, we made Wes's week, and so far"—she crossed her fingers— "Mrs. Tamarack hasn't shut us down."

Beatrice bumped Lenny back. "All the good parts were you."

Behind her green glasses, Lenny's cheeks turned red. "Teamwork," she said.

"And . . ." Beatrice's voice brightened. "Did you see Mrs. Tamarack took down the 'Wanted' poster?"

Lenny laughed. "I was afraid *you* did that."

"I heard someone gave Mrs. Tamarack an anonymous tip," said Sam. She twisted a flag in her fingers. "That 'Most Strict' was a compliment."

Lenny and Beatrice stared at the newest member of their group. Sam had their full attention again.

A tiny smile touched her lips.

"I also heard the anonymous tip was written on a typewriter," she said, with a nod toward her room. "Kind of like that one." A black machine with old-fashioned keys sat on a table just inside the window.

Sam laughed at the looks on their faces, then raised her ice cream over her head. "Bravo Zulu, guys."

Lenny and Beatrice quickly lifted theirs too. "Bravo Zulu, Sam!"

In honor of the adventure that brought them together, and all the ones to come, the three members of Operation Upside bonked their bowls in celebration.

Beatrice glanced at her friends—one old, and one new. "So," she said. "I've been thinking about who should get the next UPSIDE. . . ."

Conspiracy twinkled in Lenny's eyes. "I have ideas."

"Me too," said Sam, her smile wide.

"Me three," said Beatrice. She filled her spoon and savored a giant bite of dessert.

The trio whispered possibilities as the sun went down and the sky glowed pink all around them. Together, on Sam Darzi's roof, their future tasted as sweet as ice cream.

Acknowledgments

It's been an overwhelmingly wonderful year since *Beatrice Zinker, Upside Down Thinker* entered the world. To all the readers, teachers, librarians, friends, and booksellers who have embraced and championed Beatrice, thank you from the bottom of my heart.

To the authors, illustrators, and educators who have reached out to offer support and friendship, I'm constantly inspired by each of you and the part you play in this beautiful community.

Thank you to each school who welcomed me this year. And to the students who shared their art, their stories, and their dreams—love your weird and keep creating things that make you happy.

To my editor, Rotem Moscovich—thank you for believing in Beatrice and always helping me tell the best version of her story. Also many thanks to the Disney Hyperion team—especially Heather Crowley, Mary Claire Cruz, Amy Goppert, and Dina Sherman.

To Stephen Barr, agent and friend—I'll never stop feeling lucky and too grateful for words.

To Lisabeth, Nicole, Amy, and my sister, Shari—your friendship is a sanity-saving gift. I'm so grateful to call you friends.

To my amazing parents, and my extended family, I love you. Your love and support mean so much.

To Matthew and Nolan—you guys make life wonderful.

Finally, a million thanks to Bob, my best bud, who deserves every book dedication and all the accolades for endlessly encouraging, picking up the slack, and keeping the caffeine and candy coming.

ALPHA

BRAVO

CHARLIE

GOLF

HOTEL

KILO

LIMA

MIKE

QUEBEC

ROMEO

UNIFORM

VICTOR

WHISKEY